play it again, Charlie Brown

play it again

by Charles M. Schul

Charlie Brown

WORLD PUBLISHING
TIMES MIRROR
NEW YORK

Published by The World Publishing Company
Published simultaneously in Canada
by Nelson, Foster & Scott Ltd.
First printing—1971
Copyright © 1971 by United Feature Syndicate, Inc.
Produced in association with
Lee Mendelson—Bill Melendez TV Production
Illustrations from the Lee Mendelson—Bill Melendez
television production "Play It Again, Charlie Brown"
All rights reserved
Library of Congress catalog card number: 76-169253
Printed in the United States of America

WORLD PUBLISHING
TIMES MIRROR

Lucy had always liked Schroeder, but some-how found it impossible to impress him. Schroeder seemed interested only in playing his piano. Some days while he was practicing, Lucy would walk into the room, lounge on one end of the little piano, and try to think about how nice it would be if Schroeder liked her as much as she liked him.

Sometimes, of course, she came up with some pretty weird thoughts. "I'll bet I know something you don't know, Schroeder."

"What's that?" he asked.

Lucy got up from the piano, walked out of the room . . .

. . . and then quickly returned.

"Beethoven now comes in spray cans."

That afternoon, Lucy was talking to Sally, Charlie Brown's little sister, and she said, "I've tried everything, but I can't get Schroeder to notice me."

"Here comes Peppermint Patty," said Sally. "She always seems to come up with answers to problems. Maybe she can help."

"What's with you, Lucille?" asked Peppermint Patty. "You look down in the dumps." Peppermint Patty always had a way of calling people by names which were a little different from the names other people used.

"Oh, she is trying to get Schroeder to pay
some attention to her," explained Sally.

"Schroeder? He's the kid who is always banging away at his piano, right? Well, look, Lucille, I think I can solve your problem and you can help me at the same time." Peppermint Patty always seemed to have fantastic solutions for difficult problems like these.

"The PTA is giving a big benefit, and I am supposed to line up talent. I'll tell you what. I'll fix it up so Schroeder will get to make his professional debut. That ought to make you a hero with him.

Just leave it up to me, Lucille. You tell your lover-
boy that it's all set."

Lucy ran off happily to tell Schroeder this
good news, but she knew that she had to break
it rather gently in order to get him to listen to her.
"Schroeder?" she asked . . .

. . ."What would you think of a person if that person could do a great favor for another person?"

Schroeder said, "I would think he was a very nice person."

"OK, then," said Lucy. "What would you think if I could have you perform your ol' Beethoven in front of a huge audience?

In other words, I have just signed you up to play
for the PTA benefit show."

"I can't believe it," said Schroeder. "That's very nice. Thank you. I'd better start practicing right away."

Lucy got up and walked outside in sort of a daze.

"He said 'thank you'. He said 'thank you' to me. He said 'thank you'."

She bumped into Snoopy and gave him a big hug. "He said 'thank you'."

She saw Charlie Brown and also threw her arms around him, giving him a big hug. "He said 'thank you'. He said 'thank you' to me. He actually said 'thank you'."

"It worked, Patty. He said 'thank you' to me."

"That's great, Lucille. Oh, by the way, I better mention it now. Make sure that Schroeder doesn't play any of that Beethoven stuff. This is going to be a rock concert, and I am afraid that ol' Beethoven won't fit into the program."

"I'm doomed!" said Lucy to herself. "Schroeder will never understand. Beethoven is his hero, and he will never play in a rock concert."

She tried to explain this to Charlie Brown and Pig-Pen and Snoopy;

and Snoopy immediately
came up with a suggestion.

In a matter of moments he had
gathered up a set of drums, an
electric guitar, and a bass.

After a brief demonstration, Lucy was convinced that this little combo might be just the kind of background that Schroeder might be willing to accompany.

"Why, Schroeder," she said. "Look what I found. A combo for your concert."

"Combo?" exclaimed Schroeder. "Who asked for a combo?"

"You've got to have some backing," said Lucy.
"Aren't they great?"

"Forget it, Lucy.

I appreciate it, but Beethoven
and I can handle it alone."

"But, Schroeder," said Lucy,

"I just found out they won't
allow Beethoven. They're
expecting a rock concert."

"Well, if that's the way they feel," said Schroeder, "just tell them to forget it."

By this time, of course, Snoopy, Charlie Brown, and Pig-Pen were all set to perform, and they couldn't understand why Schroeder didn't want to play with them. Peppermint Patty had everything set up on the stage at the school, and the people in the audience were waiting for the performers to appear.

"I just can't go through with it," said Schroeder. "If I played with this combo, Beethoven would never forgive me.

I'd feel as if I were selling out. I'm sorry, Patty, but a person has to do the things he believes in."

"This is terrible!" said Peppermint Patty. "What will I do now?

The PTA is left without a program."

"Don't worry, Patty," said Lucy. "You tried to help me. Now I think I can help you." She left the stage for a moment and then quickly returned. She had a small object in her hand and when she pressed the button on top, some strange words came out. "The meeting of the PTA will come to order. We will dispense with the minutes of the last meeting. We will now have the treasurer's report."

"PTA programs also come in spray cans," said Lucy.